GOODNIGHT MOON

by Margaret Wise Brown
Pictures by Clement Hurd

HARPERCOLLINS*PUBLISHERS*

In the great green room
There was a telephone
And a red balloon
And a picture of—

The cow jumping over the moon

And there were three little bears sitting on chairs

And two little kittens
And a pair of mittens

And a little toyhouse
And a young mouse

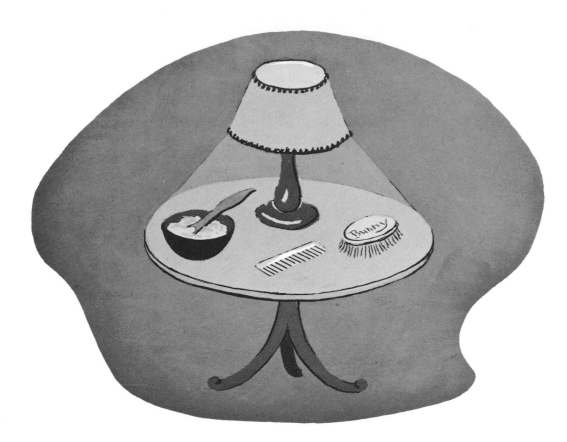

And a comb and a brush and a bowl full of mush

And a quiet old lady who was whispering "hush"

Goodnight room

Goodnight moon

Goodnight cow jumping over the moon

Goodnight light
And the red balloon

Goodnight bears
Goodnight chairs

Goodnight kittens

And goodnight mittens

Goodnight clocks
And goodnight socks

Goodnight little house

And goodnight mouse

Goodnight comb
And goodnight brush

Goodnight nobody

Goodnight mush

And goodnight to the old lady
whispering "hush"

Goodnight stars

Goodnight air

Goodnight noises everywhere